# MY FAMILY VACATION

## VACATION

### DAYAL

### KAUR

### KHALSA

CLARKSON N. POTTER, INC./PUBLISHERS

*For*
*Shirley*

**M**ay woke up when it was still dark out. She helped Dad pack the car just as dawn was breaking. May was getting ready to go on her first family vacation—to Florida.

**A**s Dad pulled into the gas station to fill the tank for the long drive ahead, it started to snow. "We're not leaving a minute too soon," he said.

May felt exactly the opposite. She stuck her head out the window and caught a snowflake on her tongue. "I love snow!" she yelled. "I don't want to go."

"Don't be stupid," said her big brother, Richie. "We'll only be away a few weeks. It will still be winter when we get back."

"Please don't call your sister stupid," Mom told him. "All this is very new to her."

They drove all day and far into the night. "I want to put as many miles between the snow and us as I can," Dad explained.

May couldn't understand that at all. So far she hadn't seen anything as good as snow.

"Just wait until we get to Florida," Mom said. "You'll forget all about snow."

**W**hen they got to the motel that night May was so excited she couldn't fall asleep. She had never slept away from home before. She loved everything about the place—from the big bouncy beds to the paper covers on the drinking glasses to the writing paper and envelopes in the night-table drawer. The miniature bars of soap, though, were her favorites. She took them all as souvenirs.

"You're such a baby," sneered Richie. "It's just a bunch of soap."

But May knew it was very special soap. "It's vacation soap," she told him.

May and Richie spent the next day's drive seeing who could count the most trucks.

Suddenly May sniffed hard. "I smell burning rubber," she said.

"You're nuts," said Richie.

 few minutes later wisps of blue smoke came streaming out from under the hood of the car. Dad stopped and they all got out.

"Where are we?" asked May.

Mom looked at the map. "Right smack in the middle of nowhere."

**L**ater that day a farmer towed the car to the nearest garage. The mechanic said it was beyond repair.

Dad had to buy a used car. To celebrate, the salesman bought everyone ice-cream cones. He gave May and Richie each a souvenir—a key chain with a little license plate with his name stamped on it in gold.

**M**ay loved souvenirs. They were her favorite part of the trip. She bought postcards at almost every stop. She took a little sugar pack and a paper place mat from all the restaurants. The backseat was getting very full.

**T**he weather grew warm. By the time they stopped for lunch, they didn't even need sweaters.

Richie bet May that he could eat his watermelon faster than she could. May tried her best to beat him. She even swallowed the seeds. But, as usual, Richie won.

**T**he motel they stayed at that day had a swimming pool. May dared Richie to jump off the diving board.

"I dare you back," he snapped.

Richie went first. He climbed onto the little board, ran to the end, and jumped off into the pool as if it were nothing.

May was just climbing onto the board for her turn when Mom called that it was time to get dressed for supper.

"Lucky for you, scaredy-cat," teased Richie.

"I am not a scaredy-cat!" said May. "I'll show you tomorrow."

But the next day there was no time to go to the pool. Right after breakfast Dad announced, "Sight-seeing today. Everyone into the car!"

Richie whispered in May's ear, "Next time."

The things they did that day were so interesting, May forgot all about the dare.

**T**hey went on a boat that had portholes under the water. They were so close to the fish that May felt as if she were swimming right along with them. Afterward she bought two postcards of people waterskiing.

In the afternoon they went to the Parrot Jungle. Big macaws and cockatoos whistled at them, and screamed, "Hello, Joe," and "Hiya, Baby!" from every tree.

May added five parrot feathers to her souvenir collection.

**T**hey got back in the car again for the long drive down to Miami Beach. Richie was bored. "There are just so many cars you can count," he complained. "I love counting cars," said May.

Richie punched her. May punched him back. Mom said to Dad, "I can't wait to get to the hotel so they'll have other children to play with."

The hotel was very big. A bellhop carried their suitcases up to their suite. May quickly collected the little bars of soap from the bathroom.

May and Richie changed into bathing suits and took the elevator down to the pool.

There was the tallest diving tower they had ever seen. May wondered if Richie remembered the dare.

Richie stared at the high diving board for a long time. Then he turned to May. "I double dare you," he hissed. "Jump from the top."

May was brave but that diving board was very, very high—even for an adult. At every single step on the way up she told herself, "I am not afraid, I am not afraid."

When she got to the top, she walked out to the end of the long narrow diving board and looked down at the glittering turquoise pool below. It was so far away! She felt very, very small. But then she saw Richie, who was always winning everything, waving up at her. May took a deep breath, closed her eyes, held her nose—and jumped off.

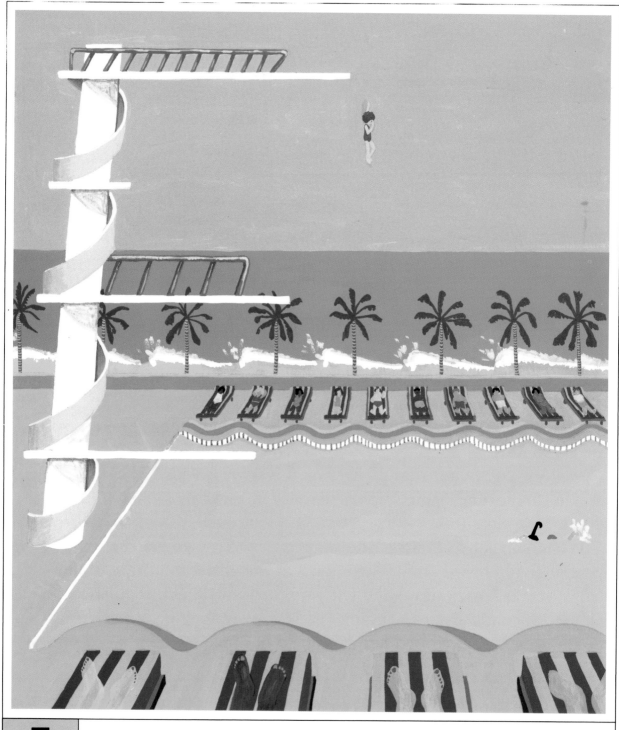

I t seemed as if she were falling forever. Richie was really impressed. He never called her a baby or a scaredy-cat again.

The hotel had a social director especially for children. She taught them games and arts and crafts. May and Richie hid whenever they saw her coming.

**W**e don't want to sit around playing a bunch of dumb games," said Richie. "We want to go places."

But Mom and Dad just wanted to lie beside the pool all day.

"I saw some interesting places right near the hotel," Dad said. "How would you like to go sight-seeing on your own?"

**T**hat suited May and Richie just fine. They had a great time together.

They went to a penny arcade and played ski ball with a sailor and a manicurist from Chicago.

**T**hey went bowling in an alley that usually didn't allow children. "But since you two look like big spenders from the North," said the manager, "I'll skip the rules today."

**T**hey played miniature golf among the palm trees.

"First one to get hit on the head by a coconut loses," said Richie.

He asked the owner if his sister could keep the little yellow scoring pencil as a souvenir.

**O**n their last night at the hotel the whole family went to a nightclub. May drank pineapple juice out of a real coconut. She took all the little pink paper umbrellas from the drinks as souvenirs of that night.

**T**he next morning May helped pack the car for the long drive home.

They drove and drove. Richie bet May that he could count the most sports cars, but she was too busy sorting out her souvenir collection to play.

The first night they put on their sweaters. The next day they put on their jackets. And the next day they put on their scarves and mittens.

"It will be nice to sleep in our own beds again," said Dad.

"And May has enough soap to last us until our next vacation," said Mom.

That night they pulled into their driveway. May was surprised to see the snow. She had forgotten all about it.

"But I'll never forget my family vacation," she said, and hurried into the house to arrange her souvenirs.

Published by Clarkson N. Potter, Inc., 201 East 50th Street, New York,
New York 10022, and distributed by Crown Publishers, Inc.

CLARKSON N. POTTER, POTTER, and colophon are trademarks
of Clarkson N. Potter, Inc.

Manufactured in Japan

Library of Congress Cataloging-in-Publication Data

Khalsa, Dayal Kaur.
My family vacation / Dayal Kaur Khalsa.
p.  cm.
Summary: Excited May takes her first trip away from home when the
family goes on vacation in Florida, and the adventures she and her
older brother have in Miami bring them to a better understanding of
each other.
[I. Miami (Fla.)—Fiction.  2. Florida—Fiction.  3. Vacations—
Fiction.  4. Brothers and sisters—Fiction.]  I. Title.
PZ7.K52647My  1988
[E]—dc19                                                    87-25842
                                                              CIP
                                                               AC

ISBN 0-517-56697-4
10 9 8 7 6 5 4 3 2

BOMC offers recordings and compact discs, cassettes
and records. For information and catalog write to
BOMR, Camp Hill, PA 17012.

Road

Big
Rock
where
Bob Cat hid

Squidgie-squodgie
mucky mud
with a pool
of
water

Smaller one that he stepped on.
on page 18.

Sammie Littletail's footprints

# Uncle Wiggily
## and the Sugar Cookie

by Howard R. Garis

Illustrated by Aldren Watson

Platt & Munk, Publishers/New York

**A Division of Grosset & Dunlap**

Once upon a time, Uncle Wiggily set out in search of
an adventure. On his way out the door of the hollow
stump bungalow, Nurse Jane Fuzzy Wuzzy, the dear
muskrat lady, stopped him.

"While you are out looking for adventure, Uncle Wiggily, I'd like you to pick up something at the store. And for fear you may forget it, I have written the name of it on this sugar cookie."

"Ha! What a very good idea!" chuckled Uncle Wiggily, as he put it in his pocket. "I'll be sure to remember. Good-bye for awhile!"

And away he hopped, over the fields and through the woods. All of a sudden, he heard a rustling in the bushes.

"Why, Sammie Littletail!" cried Uncle Wiggily. "What are you doing here?"

"I'm looking for a mud puddle," answered Sammie.

"A mud puddle! Whatever for?" cried the rabbit gentleman.

"I just got these new rubber boots, and I want to test them for leaks."

Into the meadow hopped Uncle Wiggily and
Sammie, and, sure enough, there was just the nicest
mud puddle for which a heart could wish. It was all
squidgie-squodgie, mucky mud, with a pool of water
at the center.

As Uncle Wiggily watched Sammie wading out from shore, he reached into his pocket for the cookie. But just as he took a bite, he saw the pink candy letters.

"You're doing ever so well, Sammie," he said. "But
I just remembered I have to go to the store for
Nurse Jane. Wait here until I come back."
And away hopped Uncle Wiggily.

Just as Uncle Wiggily made his purchase at the store,
Mrs. Moo Cow came running in, crying:
"Hurry, Uncle Wiggily. Hurry and help Sammie!

He's stuck in the mud puddle with his new boots,
and he can't get out!" mooed Mrs. Cow.
    Uncle Wiggily ran to the rescue.

"Sammie!" cried Uncle Wiggily. "Jump out of your boots and wade over here in your stocking feet."

"No! No, indeed!" cried Sammie. "Do you think I'm going to leave my new boots stuck in the mud? I won't come out unless they do."

Uncle Wiggily held out a fence rail across the mud
puddle. Sammie grasped it in his front paws. There
was a long strong pull. There was a squidgie-squodgie
sound, as the boots and the rabbit boy in them were
pulled out of the sticky mud.

Sammie giggled and blushed.

"At least my boots don't leak. Thank you, Uncle Wiggily! But, oh, Uncle Wiggily, look what's coming! Look! Look!" cried Sammie.

Out from behind a big rock came the bad Bob Cat
and caught Uncle Wiggily. "I want ears!" he howled.

"Excuse me," said Uncle Wiggily, "but your claws need cutting!" And taking from his pocket the long pair of scissors which he had bought for Nurse Jane, he began to trim the bad Bob Cat's nails.

The bad Bob Cat was so terrified (no one had ever before trimmed his nails) that he ran off into the woods and didn't come back for a long, long time.

And so Uncle Wiggily drove away the Bad Chap that tried to nibble his ears, and everything came out all right, for which I am very thankful, and I hope you are, too.

Then he helped Sammie wash the mud off his new boots and gave the rabbit boy a piece of the sugar cookie he had saved. And that's the end of the story. And if the bathtub doesn't go downstairs and stay out on the front porch to scare the milkman when he brings us the chocolate cake, I'll be back to tell you another adventure.